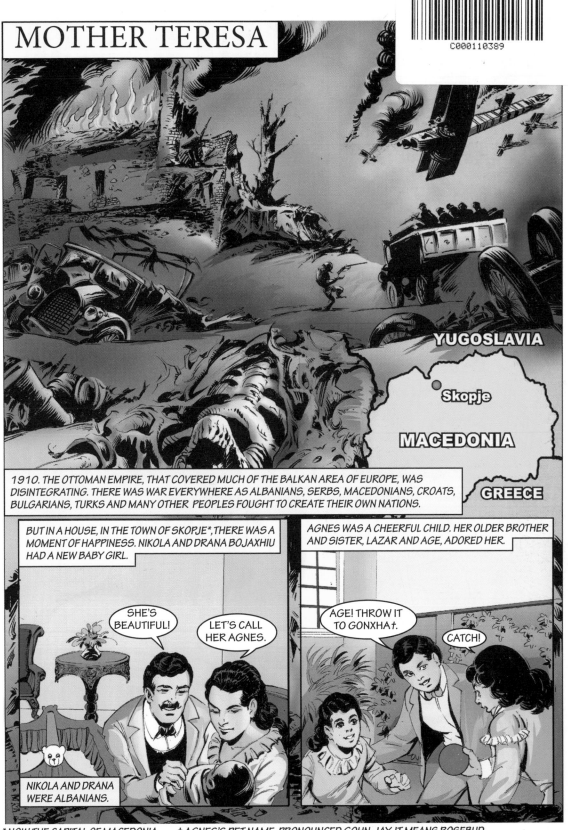

MOTHER TERESA

YUGOSLAVIA

Skopje

MACEDONIA

GREECE

1910. THE OTTOMAN EMPIRE, THAT COVERED MUCH OF THE BALKAN AREA OF EUROPE, WAS DISINTEGRATING. THERE WAS WAR EVERYWHERE AS ALBANIANS, SERBS, MACEDONIANS, CROATS, BULGARIANS, TURKS AND MANY OTHER PEOPLES FOUGHT TO CREATE THEIR OWN NATIONS.

BUT IN A HOUSE, IN THE TOWN OF SKOPJE*, THERE WAS A MOMENT OF HAPPINESS. NIKOLA AND DRANA BOJAXHIU HAD A NEW BABY GIRL.

SHE'S BEAUTIFUL!

LET'S CALL HER AGNES.

NIKOLA AND DRANA WERE ALBANIANS.

AGNES WAS A CHEERFUL CHILD. HER OLDER BROTHER AND SISTER, LAZAR AND AGE, ADORED HER.

AGE! THROW IT TO GONXHA†.

CATCH!

* NOW THE CAPITAL OF MACEDONIA.   † AGNES'S PET NAME. PRONOUNCED GOHN-JAY. IT MEANS ROSEBUD.

AGNES GREW UP TO BE A THOUGHTFUL CHILD. ONE NIGHT –

CLINK

I WONDER WHO'S UP SO LATE?

LAZAR, IT'S PAST MIDNIGHT AND YOU ARE HERE EATING JAM!

ARE YOU GOING TO TELL NANA*?

NO. BUT YOU SHOULD STOP BY YOURSELF. BESIDES, WE HAVE TO BE UP EARLY TOMORROW FOR MASS.

LAZAR WAS, OF COURSE, SLEEPY IN CHURCH!

BUT THEY THAT WAIT UPON THE LORD, SHALL RENEW THEIR STRENGTH.

LAZAR WOULD SOMETIMES MAKE FUN OF THE PRIEST.

LET'S ALL WAIT AND WAIT AND WAIT....

LAZAR, DON'T! WE MUST RESPECT OUR PRIEST.

AGNES IS RIGHT, SON. DO TRY AND FOLLOW HER EXAMPLE.

PERHAPS DRANA GUESSED THE PERSON AGNES WOULD BECOME.

NIKOLA TRAVELLED A LOT ON BUSINESS BUT THE TIME HE SPENT AT HOME, WAS FULL OF FUN AND LAUGHTER.

PULL OUT ALL THE MATCHBOXES YOU HAVE AND PILE THEM UP HERE!

KOLE, WHAT ARE YOU DOING?

HA! HA! BUILDING A BONFIRE. IT'S COLD, DRANA!

DRANA AND NIKOLA OFTEN HELPED THEIR NEIGHBOURS WHO WERE IN NEED.

HURRY, GONXHA, WE HAVE TO GO SEE HALLË* ALKETA. SHE'S SICK AGAIN.

THIS WILL HELP YOU SLEEP, ALKETA.

POOR BABY, YOUR MOTHER WILL SOON BE BETTER.

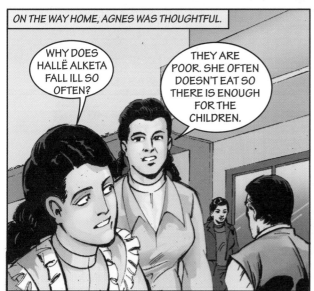

ON THE WAY HOME, AGNES WAS THOUGHTFUL.

WHY DOES HALLË ALKETA FALL ILL SO OFTEN?

THEY ARE POOR. SHE OFTEN DOESN'T EAT SO THERE IS ENOUGH FOR THE CHILDREN.

AGNES COULD NOT IMAGINE WHAT IT WAS LIKE TO GO WITHOUT FOOD.

THERE MUST BE SO MANY WHO SUFFER LIKE THIS. I WISH I COULD DO SOMETHING FOR THEM.

*SIMILAR TO 'AUNTY'

NIKOLA WAS KEEN THAT HIS DAUGHTERS GOT AS GOOD AN EDUCATION AS HIS SON.

YOU SHOULD STUDY NOW, AGNES. YOU WON'T REALISE HOW IMPORTANT IT IS UNTIL YOU'RE MUCH OLDER.

I WILL, BABA. I WANT TO BE A TEACHER WHEN I GROW UP.

GOOD! YOU CAN HELP THOSE WHO AREN'T AS LUCKY AS YOU.

NIKOLA'S WORK AND TRAVEL KEPT HIM IN TOUCH WITH POLITICS. ONE DAY –

DRANA, I'M LEAVING FOR BELGRADE TOMORROW. THERE IS A MEETING TO DISCUSS ALBANIAN INDEPENDENCE.

THAT NIGHT, AS ALWAYS, THE FAMILY GATHERED TO PRAY TOGETHER.

THIS IS MY FAVOURITE TIME OF DAY, WHEN WE'RE ALL TOGETHER.

FAMILY PRAYER TIME WAS A PRECIOUS MEMORY THAT AGNES CARRIED WITH HER ALL HER LIFE.

THE NEXT MORNING, NIKOLA LEFT FOR BELGRADE.

I WANT TO COME TOO!

YOU WILL, WHEN THE WAR IS OVER.

SEE YOU IN A WEEK, BABA!

THE FAMILY DID NOT SUSPECT THAT TRAGEDY WOULD SOON BEFALL THEM.

EVEN TODAY, NO ONE KNOWS EXACTLY WHAT HAPPENED TO NIKOLA.

AGNES HURRIED TO THE CHURCH.

IS THE PRIEST HERE? MY FATHER IS VERY ILL.

I'M SORRY, HE IS AWAY.

I SAW A PRIEST WAITING AT THE RAILWAY STATION, A WHILE AGO.

I HOPE HE IS STILL THERE.

AGNES FOUND THE PRIEST.

PLEASE, WILL YOU COME TO OUR HOUSE? MY FATHER IS VERY ILL!

I HAVE A TRAIN TO CATCH, CHILD.

BUT OUR PRIEST ISN'T HERE AND NANA SAYS WE MUST HAVE A PRIEST!

THE PRIEST COULD NOT REFUSE AGNES.

YEA, THOUGH I WALK THROUGH THE VALLEY OF THE SHADOW OF DEATH, I SHALL FEAR NO EVIL.*

THEY TOOK NIKOLA TO THE HOSPITAL BUT HE DIED THE NEXT DAY. AGNES WAS ONLY EIGHT YEARS OLD.

ALL THE PEOPLE NIKOLA AND DRANA HAD HELPED, CAME TO COMFORT THE FAMILY.

* A LINE FROM THE BIBLE.

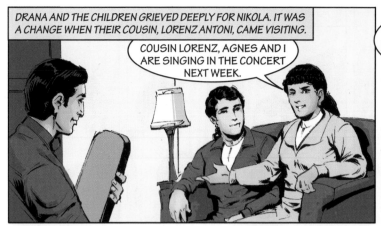

DRANA AND THE CHILDREN GRIEVED DEEPLY FOR NIKOLA. IT WAS A CHANGE WHEN THEIR COUSIN, LORENZ ANTONI, CAME VISITING.

COUSIN LORENZ, AGNES AND I ARE SINGING IN THE CONCERT NEXT WEEK.

I'LL TEACH YOU HOW TO PLAY THE MANDOLIN WITH YOUR SONG.

AGNES WAS A QUICK LEARNER.

ON THE DAY OF THE CONCERT –

DO COME, NANA. WE'RE SINGING SOME OF YOUR FAVOURITE SONGS TODAY.

I JUST DON'T FEEL UP TO IT, MY DEAR.

SHE KNEW BABA LONGER THAN WE DID. CAN YOU IMAGINE HOW SAD SHE MUST BE?

WITH DRANA SO DESPONDENT, IT WAS AGE WHO LOOKED AFTER AGNES AND LAZAR.

LORD, MAKE ME AN INSTRUMENT OF THY PEACE....

THEY SING SO BEAUTIFULLY!

LIKE NIGHTINGALES.

THIS SONG, THE PRAYER OF ST FRANCIS OF ASSISI, WOULD ALWAYS BE AGNES' FAVOURITE.

THE MONTHS PASSED. DRANA STILL MISSED NIKOLA TERRIBLY.

CHEER UP, NANA.

JUST THEN –

BABA'S PARTNER HAS TAKEN ALL THE MONEY FROM THEIR BUSINESS! NANA, WHAT WILL WE LIVE ON?

I'LL THINK OF SOMETHING, CHILDREN. DON'T WORRY.

DRANA STARTED A BUSINESS IN CLOTH.

SO MANY PEOPLE ARE BUYING YOUR EMBROIDERY, NANA!

IT'S GOOD WORK. IT'S NOT HEROIC BUT I MAKE SURE YOU CHILDREN CAN LIVE COMFORTABLY.

THAT IS WHAT ST THERESÉ SAYS TOO. EVEN THE SMALLEST WORK IS GOOD, AS LONG AS YOU DO IT WITH LOVE.

ST THERESÉ IS THE PATRON SAINT OF MISSIONARIES. HER LIFE INSPIRED AGNES.

DESPITE HER WORK, DRANA STILL MADE TIME TO HELP WHOEVER SHE COULD.

TRY AND EAT A LITTLE, FILÉ. WHAT'S THE USE OF MY COMING HERE IF YOU WON'T EAT?

IT'S NOT THE FOOD. JUST YOUR BEING HERE MAKES ME FEEL BETTER.

WHAT MAKES FILÉ REALLY SUFFER IS LONELINESS. NANA AND I CANNOT CURE HER SICKNESS BUT WE CAN MAKE SURE SHE FEELS LOVED AND WANTED.

EVERY YEAR, THE FAMILY WENT ON A TRIP TO A SHRINE IN LETNICE, IN MONTENEGRO.

DURING ONE SUCH VISIT -

I WANT TO BECOME A MISSIONARY. I WANT TO HELP PEOPLE FAR AWAY. GUIDE ME, MOTHER. LET ME DO WHAT IS RIGHT.

AGNES WAS NOW 12.

SIX YEARS PASSED -

I'M GOING TO THE CHURCH LIBRARY. THE NEW PRIEST, FATHER JAMBRENKOVIC, HAS ARRANGED A TALK BY A MISSIONARY* WHO WORKED IN INDIA!

HIS WORK IS SO INSPIRING!

TELL ME, CAN I GO AS A MISSIONARY TO INDIA, FATHER JAMBREKOVIC!

IT WILL BE VERY HARD. YOU WILL HAVE TO LEAVE HOME FOREVER. ARE YOU SURE THE THOUGHT OF THIS WORK MAKES YOU HAPPY?

YES! YES, IT DOES MAKE ME HAPPY.

APPLY TO THE LORETO ORDER, THEN. THEY HAVE A MISSION IN INDIA.

THE LORETO ORDER IS A GROUP OF MISSIONARIES WHO TEACH CHILDREN ALL OVER THE WORLD. THEY HAVE MANY SCHOOLS IN INDIA.

*A MISSIONARY IS ONE WHO IS SENT TO DO RELIGIOUS OR CHARITABLE WORK IN ANOTHER COUNTRY OR TERRITORY.

FILLED WITH PURPOSE, AGNES HURRIED HOME TO HER MOTHER.

I'VE DECIDED TO GO TO INDIA AS A MISSIONARY, NANA LOKE.* I WILL BE SORRY TO LEAVE YOU BUT I FEEL I MUST DO THIS.

A MISSIONARY? IN INDIA? LET ME THINK ABOUT THIS, GONXHA.

DRANA LOCKED HERSELF INTO HER ROOM AND PRAYED.

I ONLY WANT AGNES TO BE HAPPY. BUT HOW DO I KNOW WHAT'S BEST FOR HER?

THE NEXT DAY, DRANA CAME OUT OF HER ROOM, CALM AND COMPOSED. AGNES WAS WAITING AT THE DOOR.

YOU ARE DOING THE BEST THING THAT YOU CAN, GONXHA, MY ROSEBUD. PUT YOUR HAND IN GOD'S HAND AND WALK ALL THE WAY.

AGNES APPLIED TO THE LORETO ORDER AND WAS ACCEPTED.

THEY SAY I HAVE TO GO TO IRELAND AND LEARN ENGLISH. ONLY THEN WILL I BE SENT TO INDIA.

AGE TOO AGREED WITH AGNES' DECISION...

... BUT LAZAR, WHO WAS STUDYING ABROAD, DID NOT.

I DON'T LIKE YOU THROWING AWAY YOUR LIFE LIKE THIS.

AGNES WAS RESOLUTE.

DRANA AND AGE WENT TO ZAGREB TO SEE AGNES OFF.

GOOD BYE! I WILL ALWAYS REMEMBER AND LOVE YOU ALL.

ALWAYS LOOK AHEAD, AGNES. IF YOU LOOK BACK, YOU WILL TURN BACK.

AGNES NEVER SAW HER FAMILY AGAIN. SHE WAS JUST 18 YEARS OLD.

*AGNES LIKED TO CALL HER MOTHER 'NANA LOKE', MEANING 'MOTHER OF MY HEART'. LEAVING DRANA WAS ONE OF THE HARDEST THINGS SHE HAD TO DO.

AGNES SPENT TWO MONTHS IN IRELAND, LEARNING ENGLISH. FROM THERE SHE TRAVELLED TO INDIA, HALF A WORLD AWAY. IN CALCUTTA –

I COULD NEVER IMAGINE PEOPLE LIVING LIKE THIS. THERE IS SO MUCH POVERTY, SO MUCH ILLNESS.

YOU WILL FEEL BETTER WHEN WE GET TO THE CONVENT IN DARJEELING TOMORROW. THAT'S MUCH QUIETER.

AFTER CALCUTTA, IT WAS A RELIEF TO BE IN THE COOL HILLS OF DARJEELING. AT THE LORETO CONVENT –

NAMASTE.

NAMASTE.

AGNES WANTED TO ASK THE WOMAN WHO WAS SWEEPING, HER NAME …

… BUT SHE DID NOT KNOW HOW TO.

KNOWING ENGLISH MEANS I CAN SPEAK TO THE OTHER NUNS. BUT I STILL CANNOT TALK WITH THE LOCAL PEOPLE.

AGNES EARNESTLY STARTED LEARNING HINDI AND BENGALI.

IN 1931, AGNES TOOK HER FIRST VOWS AS A SISTER. SHE ALSO TOOK A NEW NAME.

I WILL BE SISTER TERESA, AFTER ST THERESÉ WHO FIRST INSPIRED ME TO BE A MISSIONARY.

THERE WAS ALREADY A SISTER THERESÉ IN THE LORETO CONVENT, SO SHE WAS CALLED 'THE BENGALI TERESA', BECAUSE SHE KNEW THE LANGUAGE SO WELL.

SISTER TERESA TAUGHT AT THE CONVENT AND WAS A POPULAR TEACHER.

IT'S EASY TO REMEMBER ITALY. IT IS THE ONE SHAPED LIKE A BOOT!

THOUGH SISTER TERESA'S STUDENTS LOVED HER CLASSES, SHE FELT SHE COULD DO MORE TO HELP PEOPLE. DURING THE VACATIONS –

I HEAR THERE IS A LOCAL CLINIC FOR PEOPLE WHO CANNOT AFFORD DOCTORS. I WANT TO VOLUNTEER.

IT IS SMALL AND BADLY EQUIPPED. ARE YOU SURE?

I WILL MAKE DO AS WELL AS I CAN.

AT THE CLINIC –

WHO IS FIRST?

HE IS TOO WEAK TO STAND. I HAVE NO FOOD. IF YOU DON'T WANT HIM, I WILL JUST ABANDON HIM. THE JACKALS WILL NOT TURN UP THEIR NOSES AT HIM.

I WILL BE YOUR SECOND MOTHER.

SISTER TERESA TOOK HER FINAL VOWS IN 1937. AT THE CEREMONY IN DARJEELING, SHE MADE A SECRET PROMISE

I WILL NEVER REFUSE GOD ANYTHING HE MAY EVER ASK OF ME.

SHE WAS NOW MOTHER TERESA.

MOTHER LIVED IN THE LORETO CONVENT IN ENTALLY, CALCUTTA. SHE TAUGHT AT ST MARY'S SCHOOL, NEXT DOOR. SHE ALSO TAUGHT AT A SMALL BENGALI MEDIUM SCHOOL NAMED ST TERESA'S. ON HER FIRST DAY –

YOU CAN'T LEARN ANY-THING IN THIS DIRT!

SHE PICKED UP A BROOM AND STARTED CLEANING.

I'LL GET A BUCKET OF WATER, MISS.

THE CHILDREN HAD NEVER SEEN A TEACHER LIKE HER BEFORE. THEY CALLED HER 'MA'.

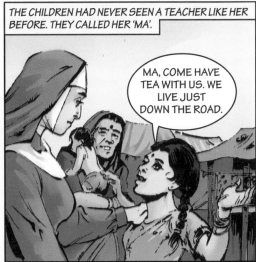

MA, COME HAVE TEA WITH US. WE LIVE JUST DOWN THE ROAD.

THIS WAS THE FIRST TIME MOTHER WAS ACTUALLY GOING INSIDE A SLUM.

HOW DO ALL OF THEM LIVE IN ONE TINY ROOM!

THESE ARE MY BROTHERS AND SISTERS.

I MUST DO SOMETHING TO HELP THESE CHILDREN.

OVER THE NEXT FEW YEARS, MOTHER BECAME MORE AND MORE ABSORBED IN THE WORK AT ST MARY'S SCHOOL. SHE STILL KEPT HEARING ABOUT HOW TERRIBLE LIFE WAS OUTSIDE THE CONVENT. WORLD WAR II WAS GOING ON. IN NEIGHBOURING BURMA, THE BRITISH FOUGHT THE JAPANESE AND REFUGEES POURED INTO CALCUTTA.

IN 1942-43, A CYCLONE HIT BENGAL, DESTROYING MANY OF THE CROPS.

THE BRITISH ARE TAKING RICE FROM INDIA TO FEED THEIR SOLDIERS. PEOPLE WILL STARVE! WE MUST DO SOMETHING.

WHAT CAN WE DO? BESIDES, IT MAY NOT BE SAFE FOR US TO GO OUTSIDE.

MOTHER TERESA COULD NOT STAND BY WITHOUT TRYING TO HELP.

IT'S NOT RIGHT THAT WE ARE PROTECTED IN HERE WHILE PEOPLE NEED HELP OUTSIDE.

WE'LL COME WITH YOU TO HELP.

WE'LL BE BACK TOMORROW. I'LL COLLECT ALL THE FOOD I CAN FIND.

IN 1944, MOTHER BECAME THE PRINCIPAL OF ST MARY'S.

THE BRITISH DECIDED TO LEAVE INDIA BUT THEY WERE GOING TO PARTITION IT INTO INDIA AND PAKISTAN. ON 16TH AUGUST 1946, HUGE RIOTS BROKE OUT IN CALCUTTA.

INSIDE THE CONVENT –

THIS IS THE LAST OF OUR FOOD.

I WILL GO OUT AND SEE WHAT I CAN DO.

THE OTHER SISTERS WERE AFRAID MOTHER TERESA WOULD GET HURT, IF SHE WENT OUTSIDE DURING THE RIOTS.

THAT DAY –

HIDE ME, PLEASE, OR THE MOB OUTSIDE WILL KILL ME.

UH!

I'LL DRESS YOUR WOUNDS AND THEN HELP YOU GO HOME.

I DON'T THINK YOU SHOULD GO OUT, MOTHER. IT'S NOT SAFE!

I CANNOT LET OUR 300 CHILDREN STARVE. LET ME GO AND FIND FOOD.

THEY WAITED FOR THE ROAD TO CLEAR.

15

THE MOB WENT THAT WAY. IF WE GO UP THE OTHER WAY, YOU CAN GET HOME AND I CAN GET FOOD.

THANK YOU! YOU SAVED MY LIFE.

MOTHER FOUND ALL THE SHOPS SHUT. JUST THEN –

WHAT ARE YOU DOING? THE MOBS ARE ATTACKING EVERYONE THEY SEE. IT'S DANGEROUS!

I CAME LOOKING FOR FOOD. THERE ISN'T ANY LEFT FOR THE CHILDREN IN THE CONVENT.

IT WAS A TRUCK FULL OF BRITISH SOLDIERS.

FOOD CAN WAIT. THIS AREA IS NOT SAFE. GET IN, WE'LL DRIVE YOU HOME.

NO. I CAN'T LET THE ENTIRE CONVENT STARVE!

THE SOLDIERS TRIED TO PER-SUADE HER TO GO BACK ...

...BUT MOTHER TERESA WAS VERY DETERMINED.

WE'LL GIVE YOU SOME OF OUR FOOD. NOW WILL YOU GET IN?

SHE GOT IN, SATISFIED.

WHEN THEY REACHED THE CONVENT -

HERE WE ARE. I DON'T KNOW IF YOU'RE VERY BRAVE OR JUST VERY STUBBORN, MOTHER.

BLESS YOU!

PEACE WAS FINALLY RESTORED BUT MOTHER TERESA WAS WEAK AND ILL.

GO TO DARJEELING FOR A FEW WEEKS AND GET SOME REST.

IT WAS ON THE TRAIN TO DARJEELING THAT SHE HEARD A VOICE.

LEAVE THE CONVENT! GIVE UP ITS COMFORT AND SAFETY. FOLLOW ME TO THE SLUMS, AMONG THE POOREST OF THE POOR.

STARTLED, MOTHER TERESA LOOKED AROUND ...

MOVE TO THE SLUMS. THIS IS YOUR TRUE VOCATION.

... BUT IT WAS CLEAR THAT THE VOICE WAS SPEAKING ONLY TO HER.

IN DARJEELING –

I HOPE MOTHER TERESA IS ALL RIGHT. USUALLY SHE'S FULL OF JOKES AND SONGS.

SHE HAS BEEN VERY QUIET. SHE JUST SITS AND WRITES ALL THE TIME!

MOTHER TERESA WAS COMPLETELY ABSORBED IN HER NEW IDEA –

In that train, I heard a call to give up all and follow Him into the slums.... It is a call within a call.

God said to me, "Come, be my light" and I go.

BACK IN CALCUTTA, MOTHER TERESA WENT STRAIGHT TO FATHER VAN EXEM.

FATHER, I NEED YOUR ADVICE. I BELIEVE I HEARD A CALL TO LEAVE THE CONVENT.

THAT IS A VERY BIG STEP TO TAKE. ARE YOU QUITE CERTAIN?

HE WAS CONVINCED BY MOTHER'S SINCERITY –

I THIRST TO DEDICATE MY LIFE TO THE POOREST OF THE POOR, FATHER, TO LIVE AS THEY DO.

THIS ISN'T WITHIN MY POWER. WRITE TO THE ARCHBISHOP OF CALCUTTA FOR GUIDANCE.

MOTHER WROTE TO THE ARCHBISHOP AND HE CALLED FATHER VAN EXEM TO DISCUSS THE LETTER.

I BELIEVE THAT SERVING THE POOR IS A GENUINE VOCATION FOR MOTHER TERESA. SHE WILL WORK WITH FAITH AND DEDICATION.

IT'S NOT SAFE FOR HER TO WANDER AROUND ALONE. I NEED AT LEAST A YEAR TO DECIDE.

THE ARCHBISHOP SAYS YOU MUST STAY IN THE CONVENT FOR A YEAR. HE NEEDS TIME TO DECIDE. BE PATIENT.

OBEDIENT TO THE ARCHBISHOP, MOTHER STAYED IN THE CONVENT, THOUGH SHE LONGED TO BE ON THE STREETS.

IT WAS AUGUST 15TH, 1947 AND INDIA BECAME INDEPENDENT. WITH INDEPENDENCE CAME PARTITION…

… AND WITH PARTITION CAME HUNGER AND HOMELESS-NESS. CALCUTTA'S STREETS WERE FULL OF REFUGEES.

MOTHER TERESA WAS HORRIFIED BY THE MISERY OUTSIDE.

INDIA IS GOING THROUGH DAYS OF HATRED. THE CITY IS FULL OF SUFFERING. YOU SHOULD ALL TRY AND HELP THOSE LESS FORTUNATE.

WE ARE READY TO HELP. BUT WE NEED A LEADER.

WHY CAN'T YOU BE OUR LEADER?

I CAN'T, SUBHASHINI, MAGDALENA. YOU KNOW I MUST WAIT FOR NOW.

MOTHER WAS STILL WAITING FOR PERMISSION TO LEAVE THE CONVENT.

AS SHE WAITED, MOTHER TERESA WAS HAUNTED BY HER CALL. A POWERFUL VISION SWEPT ACROSS HER MIND. ONE IN WHICH MARY, THE MOTHER OF JESUS CHRIST, SPOKE TO HER.

TAKE CARE OF THEM – THEY ARE MINE. FEAR NOT. JESUS AND I WILL BE WITH YOU AND YOUR CHILDREN.

HER VISIONS FILLED HER WITH URGENCY. STILL, SHE WAITED FOR THE CHURCH'S PERMISSION. HER REQUEST WAS NOW WITH THE POPE*.

* THE POPE IS THE HEAD OF THE CATHOLIC CHURCH.

THEN ONE DAY, FATHER VAN EXEM CALLED HER –

THE POPE HAS WRITTEN.

EXCUSE ME FATHER, I MUST PRAY FIRST.

MOTHER TERESA SENSED IT WAS AN IMPORTANT OCCASION.

WHEN SHE WAS DONE, SHE WAS COMPOSED AS ALWAYS.

YOUR REQUEST HAS BEEN GRANTED. YOU CAN WORK OUTSIDE THE CONVENT.

FATHER, CAN I GO TO THE SLUMS RIGHT AWAY?

IT WAS AUGUST, 1948. IT HAD BEEN TWO YEARS SINCE MOTHER TERESA FIRST HEARD THE CALL.

MOTHER LEFT FOR PATNA TO TRAIN IN NURSING AND FIRST AID. HER STUDENTS AND THE OTHER SISTERS GAVE HER A TOUCHING FAREWELL.

DID MOTHER REALLY HAVE TO LEAVE US? WE MISS HER SO.

WE MISS HER TOO BUT SHE WANTS TO SERVE THE POOR. THAT IS WHAT WILL MAKE HER HAPPIEST.

FATHER VAN EXEM WENT TO MEET MOTHER IN PATNA –

I DIDN'T RECOGNISE YOU IN THAT SARI!

HA HA! BUT IT WAS YOU WHO BLESSED MY NEW SARIS. IF I HAVE TO HELP THE POOREST, I MUST LIVE LIKE THEY DO.

MOTHER HAD CHOSEN THE CHEAPEST SARI, SIMILAR TO ONE WORN BY MUNICIPAL CLEANERS, IN CALCUTTA.

MOTHER SOON FINISHED HER TRAINING. SHE WENT TO STAY WITH THE 'LITTLE SISTERS OF THE POOR' * IN CALCUTTA. ONCE THERE, SHE HEADED STRAIGHT TO A SLUM CALLED, MOTIJHEEL.

HERE ARE THE POOREST OF THE POOR, WHOM I HAVE VOWED TO HELP.

SOON, HER FIRST CLASS WAS IN FULL SWING!

KO KHO GO GHO**

* AN ORDER OF NUNS

**THE FIRST LETTERS OF THE BENGALI ALPHABET.

MORE AND MORE CHILDREN JOINED THE SCHOOL. MOTHER'S CLASSES WERE ALWAYS FUN.

REMEMBER THE CLEANEST ONE WILL GET THE BOX OF SWEETS! NOW LET'S START: ONE NOSE! WASH! TWO EARS! WASH! NOW JUMP!

SOME OF MOTHER'S OLD STUDENTS, INCLUDING MAGDALENA AND SUBHASHINI, CAME TO SEE HER.

YEARS AGO WE SAID WE'D HELP IF YOU WOULD LEAD US.

LET US JOIN YOU NOW.

THEY TOOK THEIR VOWS AS SISTER AGNES (AFTER MOTHER) AND SISTER GERTRUDE.

MOTHER WANTED THE CHILDREN TO LEARN SKILLS, USING WASTE MATERIAL. SHE AND HER SISTERS TAUGHT TOY-MAKING WITH CARDBOARD ...

ISN'T MY SOLDIER ALMOST AS GOOD AS PATRO'S?

... AND KNITTING WITH TWIGS.

UP HERE, LOOP, AND PULL, LIKE THIS!

SOON, MORE SISTERS JOINED THEM.

WITH SO MANY OF YOU HELPING, I CAN START A DISPENSARY.

FATHER VAN EXEM CAME TO VISIT THEM –

ALL THE NEW SISTERS ARE SUCH A JOY TO ME.

YOU SHOULD MOVE CLOSER TO MOTIJHEEL.

I KNOW. I'VE BEEN LOOKING FOR A NEW HOUSE.

I THINK I KNOW JUST THE PLACE.

THAT EVENING –

RETREA...

THIS IS MR GOMES. HE OWNS THIS HOUSE.

COME UPSTAIRS. I'D BE HAPPY TO GIVE YOU SPACE ON THE TOP FLOOR.

I AM AT HOME ALREADY.

THEY NOW HAD A PLACE TO STAY IN BUT THEY WERE STILL SHORT OF MONEY.

MOTHER TERESA HAD TO ASK PEOPLE FOR FOOD AND MEDICINES.

SHANTHI CHEMISTS

I NEED MORE BANDAGES FOR MY CLINIC.

I GAVE YOU LOTS YESTERDAY. BEGONE!

SHE PERSISTED –

I WAS HOPING YOU COULD GIVE ME SOME MONEY. I WANT TO START A FREE CLINIC FOR POOR PEOPLE.

I CAN GIVE YOU A HUNDRED RUPEES. WILL THAT DO?

IN THOSE DAYS A HUNDRED RUPEES WAS MORE THAN MOST PEOPLE EARNED IN FOUR MONTHS. MOTHER IMMEDIATELY USED THE MONEY TO RENT ROOMS.

ONE ROOM WAS FOR THE SCHOOL., THE OTHER WAS A SMALL DISPENSARY –

DON'T FORGET TO TAKE THE MEDICINE AFTER YOU EAT SOMETHING.

A RICH BUSINESSMAN IN MADRAS AGREED TO MEET MOTHER ABOUT DONATING FOR A SHISHU BHAVAN*. MOTHER WAS PUNCTUAL.

HE'S NOT READY YET. YOU'LL HAVE TO WAIT.

SHE WAITED A WHOLE HOUR. FINALLY –

WHAT IS IT YOU WANT?

A STREAM OF BETEL-JUICE...

...FLEW OUT...

...AND FELL ON MOTHER'S SARI.

MOTHER NEVER MINDED HUMILIATION FOR HERSELF.

THANK YOU FOR THIS GIFT. NOW WHAT ABOUT MY CHILDREN?

FORGIVE ME! I HAVE BEEN RUDE!

THE MAN DONATED GENEROUSLY. HIS GRANDCHILDREN GIVE MONEY TO THE MISSIONARIES OF CHARITY TO THIS DAY.

*CHILDREN'S HOME.

EVEN WITH MONEY, IT WAS NOT EASY. PEOPLE WERE SUSPICIOUS. THEY SPOKE IN FRONT OF HER, THINKING SHE DID NOT UNDERSTAND BENGALI.

WHAT'S THE USE OF INDEPENDENCE IF THESE WHITE FIRANGIS ARE STILL EVERYWHERE?

THEY'RE JUST HERE TO CONVERT US.

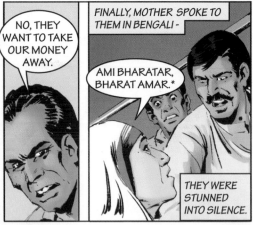

NO, THEY WANT TO TAKE OUR MONEY AWAY.

FINALLY, MOTHER SPOKE TO THEM IN BENGALI –

AMI BHARATAR, BHARAT AMAR. *

THEY WERE STUNNED INTO SILENCE.

A YEAR HAD PASSED, AND THE CHURCH HAD LET MOTHER TERESA START A NEW ORDER, THE MISSIONARIES OF CHARITY. THEIR MAIN BUILDING WAS NAMED 'MOTHER HOUSE'.

MISSIONARIES OF CHARITY
MOTHER HOUSE
54A, A. J. C. BOSE ROAD
KOLKATA - 700016

SISTER AGNES TRAINED AS A TEACHER …

MOTHER WILL INSPECT YOU AFTER CLASS. THE CLEANEST CHILD WILL GET A BOX OF SWEETS. YOU MUST SHARE IT THOUGH.

… AND SISTER GERTRUDE AS A DOCTOR. ON HER FIRST DAY –

I'M SO NERVOUS. HE'S IN SO MUCH PAIN ALREADY. I WILL ADD TO IT BY INJECTING HIM.

I'LL HOLD YOUR HAND STEADY, WE'LL INJECT HIM TOGETHER.

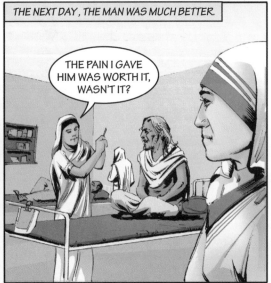

THE NEXT DAY, THE MAN WAS MUCH BETTER.

THE PAIN I GAVE HIM WAS WORTH IT, WASN'T IT?

* I AM INDIAN AND INDIA IS MINE.

FOR THOSE WHO COULD NOT BE CURED, MOTHER STARTED A HOSPICE IN KALIGHAT, IN A PLACE GIVEN TO HER BY THE GOVERNMENT. SHE CALLED IT NIRMAL HRIDAY, WHICH MEANS 'PURE HEART'.

WE WILL GIVE THEM THE BEST MEDICAL CARE!

THE BIGGEST DISEASE IS FEELING UNWANTED. WE NEED TO LOVE AND COMFORT PEOPLE IN THEIR LAST DAYS.

NEXT DOOR WAS A KALI TEMPLE. THE PRIESTS THERE WERE VERY ANGRY WITH MOTHER.

WHY DID YOU BUILD YOUR HOSPICE HERE?

THIS IS A TEMPLE.

THEN ONE OF THE PRIESTS FELL INCURABLY ILL.

IT'S TB. I'M AS GOOD AS DEAD*. BUT DON'T TRY TO FOOL ME INTO JOINING YOU.

THAT'S NOT WHY I'M HERE. YOU SHOULD BE RESTING.

SHE TOOK HIM TO NIRMAL HRIDAY. A FEW DAYS LATER –

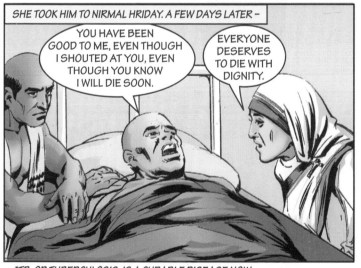

YOU HAVE BEEN GOOD TO ME, EVEN THOUGH I SHOUTED AT YOU, EVEN THOUGH YOU KNOW I WILL DIE SOON.

EVERYONE DESERVES TO DIE WITH DIGNITY.

YOU HAVE GIVEN HIM PEACE. THANK YOU.

SHE HAD WON THEIR RESPECT.

*TB, OR TUBERCULOSIS, IS A CURABLE DISEASE NOW.

MOTHER FOUND THAT THERE WAS ALWAYS SO MUCH MORE TO BE DONE.

IT'S LATE, CHILD. GO TO BED.

KNOCK

IT WAS A GROUP OF LEPERS.

WE HEARD YOU HELP THE POOREST OF THE POOR. DO YOU EVEN HELP LEPERS?

OF COURSE! COME IN.

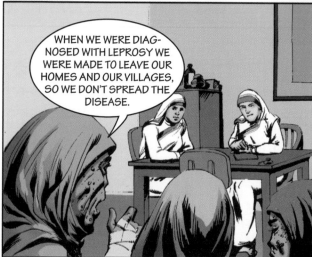

WHEN WE WERE DIAGNOSED WITH LEPROSY WE WERE MADE TO LEAVE OUR HOMES AND OUR VILLAGES, SO WE DON'T SPREAD THE DISEASE.

BUT THERE IS A MEDICINE FOR LEPROSY, NOW. IT WILL STOP THE DISEASE AND YOU CAN LIVE NORMALLY. NO ONE AROUND YOU WILL BE INFECTED.

NO ONE TOLD US, LET ALONE GAVE US MEDICINE.

PEOPLE ARE SCARED TO EVEN COME NEAR US. THEIR FEAR CLOUDS THEIR MINDS.

WE MUST DO SOMETHING!

MOTHER STARTED A COLONY CALLED SHANTI NAGAR.

THIS IS YOUR HOME NOW.

IN SHANTI NAGAR, PEOPLE WITH LEPROSY HAVE THEIR OWN HOUSES. THEY EARN A LIVING BY FARMING, SPINNING OR CARPENTRY.

MOTHER FELT THE SUFFERING AROUND HER, DEEP WITHIN HER SELF.

SO MUCH PAIN AND SORROW! WE HAVE BEEN WORKING FOR YEARS BUT IT NEVER ENDS.

BUT SHE NEVER LET THIS DARKNESS AFFECT HER WORK. SHE JUST WENT ON.

FROM 1960, MOTHER STARTED OPENING HOMES ALL OVER THE COUNTRY. A SHISHU BHAVAN WAS STARTED IN DELHI –

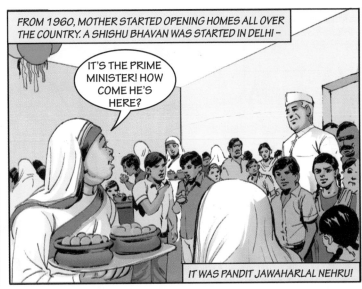

IT'S THE PRIME MINISTER! HOW COME HE'S HERE?

IT WAS PANDIT JAWAHARLAL NEHRU!

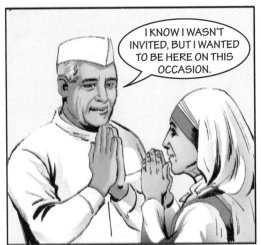

I KNOW I WASN'T INVITED, BUT I WANTED TO BE HERE ON THIS OCCASION.

WOULD YOU LIKE TO HEAR ABOUT OUR WORK?

NO. I'VE READ ALL ABOUT IT. THAT'S WHY I'M HERE.

SHE WAS FAMOUS! A FEW YEARS LATER, THE INDIAN GOVERNMENT AWARDED HER THE PADMA SHRI.

1970-71. BHOLA CYCLONE HIT EAST PAKISTAN, KILLING ALMOST 500,000 PEOPLE. LATER THAT YEAR WAR BROKE OUT THERE, AS THE PEOPLE FOUGHT TO BECOME AN INDEPENDENT COUNTRY, BANGLADESH.

WITH SO MUCH HUNGER AND DESTRUCTION, THE MISSIONARIES OF CHARITY WORKED TIRELESSLY. MOTHER OPENED HOMES IN OTHER COUNTRIES AS WELL.

THERE WAS NEVER ANY RESPITE FROM POVERTY AND SUFFERING.

AMBULANCE

I NEED A STRETCHER HERE!

I HOPE YOU'RE MORE COMFORTABLE NOW,

I HAVE LIVED LIKE AN ANIMAL BUT NOW I'LL DIE LIKE AN ANGEL!

MOTHER BELIEVED THAT BY TENDING THE SICK AND THE SUFFERING, SHE WAS SERVING JESUS CHRIST.

BY NOW, MOTHER'S WORK WAS KNOWN THROUGHOUT THE WORLD. IN 1979, SHE WON THE NOBEL PEACE PRIZE.

LOVE BEGINS AT HOME. I LEARN THAT OVER AND OVER AGAIN...

"...ONE DAY, I HEARD OF A STARVING FAMILY. I TOOK SOME FOOD AND WENT IMMEDIATELY. THEIR FACES WERE SHINING WITH HUNGER...

HERE IS SOME RICE FOR YOU ALL.

"...THE LADY DIVIDED THE RICE INTO TWO BOWLS. THEN SHE LEFT WITH ONE OF THE BOWLS.

I'LL JUST BE BACK, MOTHER.

"...I WAS PUZZLED. WHEN SHE RETURNED –"

WHERE DID YOU GO?

MY NEIGHBOURS WERE ALSO HUNGRY. I GAVE THEM SOME FOOD.

SHE WAS STARVING, BUT FELT FOR HER NEIGHBOUR'S HUNGER. THIS IS LOVE. HOW CAN WE BE ANY LESS?

THE NEXT YEAR SHE GOT INDIA'S HIGHEST CIVILIAN AWARD, THE BHARAT RATNA.

OVER THE NEXT FEW YEARS, MOTHER TERESA AND HER SISTERS WENT ALL OVER THE WORLD DOING WHAT THEY COULD TO EASE SUFFERING.

1982. THE BEIRUT WAR. STUCK IN THE MIDDLE OF THE WAR WAS A SMALL HOSPITAL WITH 37 CHILDREN IN IT. THE CHILDREN WERE MENTALLY CHALLENGED. THEY HAD NO FOOD OR WATER.

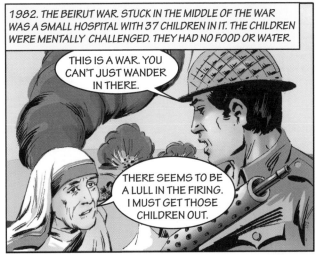

THIS IS A WAR. YOU CAN'T JUST WANDER IN THERE.

THERE SEEMS TO BE A LULL IN THE FIRING. I MUST GET THOSE CHILDREN OUT.

AN HOUR LATER –

ALL SAFE!

MOTHER HAD MANAGED THE IMPOSSIBLE.

BUT HER HARD LIFE WAS BEGINNING TO TAKE ITS TOLL ON HER BODY. A YEAR LATER, IN ROME –

YOU HAD A HEART ATTACK. THE PACEMAKER* I'VE PUT IN WILL HELP. I ADVISE YOU TO REST.

I CAN'T. I HAVE SO MUCH TO DO.

DESPITE HER WEAK HEALTH, MOTHER CONTINUED TO TRAVEL AND WORK AS BEFORE.

* A DEVICE TO HELP THE HEART BEAT NORMALLY.

BY 1997, MOTHER TERESA WAS VERY ILL.

I'M OLD AND ILL NOW. I CAN'T WORK AS WELL AS I USED TO. YOU MUST LET ME STEP DOWN AS HEAD OF THE ORDER.

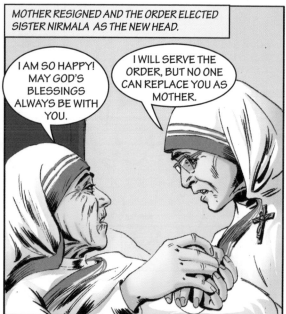

MOTHER RESIGNED AND THE ORDER ELECTED SISTER NIRMALA AS THE NEW HEAD.

I AM SO HAPPY! MAY GOD'S BLESSINGS ALWAYS BE WITH YOU.

I WILL SERVE THE ORDER, BUT NO ONE CAN REPLACE YOU AS MOTHER.

A FEW MONTHS LATER, ON SEPTEMBER 5TH, JUST AFTER FREE INDIA HAD TURNED 50 YEARS OLD, MOTHER TERESA PASSED AWAY. SHE WAS GIVEN A STATE FUNERAL WITH FULL HONOURS.

IN HER LIFETIME, MOTHER HAD SET UP 610 MISSIONS IN 123 COUNTRIES – THESE INCLUDED HOSPICES, ORPHAN-AGES, SOUP KITCHENS, SCHOOLS, AND HOMES FOR PEOPLE WITH AIDS, LEPROSY AND TB. SHE IS NOW OFFICIALLY CALLED "BLESSED TERESA OF CALCUTTA," AND THE CHURCH IS IN THE PROCESS OF DECLARING HER A SAINT.

A COLLECTOR'S EDITION,
FROM INDIA'S FAVOURITE STORYTELLER.

India's greatest epic, told over 1,300 beautifully illustrated pages.
The Mahabharata Collector's Edition. It's not just a set of books, it's a piece of culture.

AMAR CHITRA KATHA

THE MAHABHARATA
COLLECTOR'S EDITION
Rupees one thousand, nine hundred and ninety-nine only.

Vigilante